A LIFETIME TOGETHER

A LIFETIME TOGETHER

By Novoschool

Year 7, 2025

Title: A Lifetime Together
First published in 2025 by Kani Consultants,
Newcastle, Australia.
© Copyright on the text belongs to the authors.
© Copyright on the product belongs to Kani Consultants.

A catalogue record for this
work is available from the
National Library of Australia

ISBN: 978-1-7638083-6-2
Authors: Year 7 students at Novoschool, 2025
Design Assistant: Leanne Deering

Subjects:

Young adult fiction / Biographical;
Young adult fiction / Fantasy / Historical;
Young adult fiction / Biographical & Autobiographical /
Historical

Keywords:

Short stories; origin stories; anthology; secondary
students; published by students; fiction; year seven;
games; family; friends; adventure; memoir

Contents

CONTENTS

INTRODUCTION

What happens when dozens of young voices come together to tell stories that challenge, comfort, and inspire? You get a collection like no other! Crafted by budding authors who are guiding you on a journey through those formative memories and how they shaped the young people they have become, you get a chance to experience the children's perspective with many twists, turns and surprises.

This collection was created to give young voices a space to share stories that matter to them. Through the application of our school's core values, such as curiosity, global thinking, and excellence, We wanted to experience the process of creating an anthology together. Each writer brings their own unique experiences and emotions, revealing hidden thoughts and feelings. Together, these pieces create a powerful mix that reflects the diversity and strength of our generation.

This anthology is divided into three parts, each with its own unique focus and flavour:

Adventure invites readers to dive into thrilling journeys and new experiences that spark curiosity, bravery, and the excitement of discovering the unknown. From daring explorations to moments of self-discovery, these stories capture the spirit of stepping beyond your comfort zone.

Family & Friends explores the deep connections, unconditional support and sometimes complicated emotions that shape our relationships with the people we care about most. These pieces reveal the laughter, challenges, love and reality with misunderstandings that come with close bonds.

Our **Games** section celebrates imagination, fun and the valuable lessons we learn through play, teamwork and friendly competition. Through playful stories and creative expressions, this part shows how games can teach resilience, strategy and the joy of shared moments.

Inside this anthology, you'll find a collection of personal stories written straight from the heart. Each piece is based on a real moment or meaningful experience in the writer's life – some big, some small but all significant origin stories. Whether it's a challenge faced, a lesson learned, or a joyful memory held close, these stories offer a genuine glimpse into what it means to grow, change, and reflect. Every voice brings something unique, making this collection as diverse as the students who created it.

So just be aware, these aren't just words on a page. They're pieces of who we are, and now, we're sharing them with you. So take a deep breath, turn the page, and step into our world, one honest story at a time.

Bana Qattan
Student, Year 7

Section 1

Section One:
Family & Friends

The Blanket

Alexander Lindsay

I was running, never stopping. I'm chasing him, bloodthirsty for what he has obtained. Never had I ran so fast before in my life. I was losing energy, he was getting further and further away. I am still too slow to get it, how can I get the blanket back? Was I losing? And then all of a sudden, it's gone. I lost it, I was too slow, He was gone. Will was his name. I couldn't find him, he was faster than me either way, all I could do was wait for him. I found him running as fast as the wind. I stepped on it and he tripped and got stuck, I finally reclaimed my prize!! THE BLANKET!

No time to lose! Just keep running, running, running. He's still on the floor. I need to hide. I can't outrun him. But I can outsmart him. I remembered that we're moving houses. Nowhere to hide, only places to run, so much space! And then that's when it hit me. I can't run or hide. But I CAN ALWAYS FIGHT WITH THE LEFTOVER PILLOWS!

I heard him coming, so I grabbed a pillow, holding it in an almost professional grip. I had no chance of losing the blanket again. But he just so happened to have the same idea. As we met, I hit him in the head with the pillow and while staggering, falling down onto the pillows he hit my legs and got a loose grip of the blanket. But I wasn't going to let myself lose it. I tugged the blanket as hard as I could and dragged him across the floor. He let go; his shirt was pulled half off from being on the floor.

We were fighting for the blanket, not for who can use it, but just for who has it. It was on and we were showing no mercy to each other. It was a riot, no, it was a war and nothing less. I was determination itself. I was perseverance.

What happened next? They went on and on for generations. The blanket being prized more than gold to them.

But ... the war had to end. We were moving houses. No matter what we did, the war would eventually have to end. But we were still determined. We had never felt more of a desperate feeling before in our lives. Our parents were mad at us, and he had to go home. My mum didn't like me hitting Will in the head with the pillow, but eventually, we had no choice but to join forces and ... RUN AND HIDE.

Will hid under the blanket and I hid under a washing basket, but my intrusive thoughts came through, and I kept wondering, what if this is all a trick? What if my mum and Will's mum said he was going just so I had to give him the blanket so he could run away with it? What if this is all just their master plot? So, I asked him if he was tricking me about going so he could keep the blanket and he said no. So, we just carried on running and hiding. My mum and his thought Will was a ghost, and that I was a turtle!

Eventually, after running into a series of walls, we found my room. We hid under the blankets and covered ourselves in pillows. We couldn't resist hitting each other with them, until we heard our parents coming. We thought we had better be quiet and cover ourselves, so we did. When they came into the room, we could hear them asking where we were. And then ... they say the blankets. They must have thought the turtle was trapped underneath!

They pulled the blankets off and pillows and found us. We had to escape, so we kept running, ricocheting off walls as we went, until we finally found the way back to my room. After a bit of peeking around corners to make sure it was clear, we hid in the closet. But our parents had planned ahead.

They had hidden in the room, expecting us to run back, and by the time we realised their ploy, we were caught. Will was dragged away, as I hugged him, trying to stop him from being taken away, stopping him from being able to breathe in the process. His mother finally succeeded in dragging him away, and so he left. The war was over.

Autograph:

Biography:

Alex is a 12-year-old kid. He lives with a family of five: his mum, his two dogs and his cat. His favourite hobbies are gaming, tennis and ping pong!

The Day I Got My Dog

Claudia Sim

When I got my dog, it was a fabulous day. It was beautiful and sunny, I felt the warmth of the sun on my skin and the breeze on my face. It started a couple of weeks earlier in my home. Me, trying to convince my parents to buy me a dog.

I was five years old, about to start Kindergarten, and my whole family wanted a dog. Well ... almost my whole family.

Everyone except my mum.

She said that dogs are smelly, and she would have to clean up after it, but she was probably right about that. So, you know what the little five-year-old me had done, I climbed up the study chair and reached up onto the top shelf and wrapped my little fingers around the tub of pencils and paper so I could start drawing my masterpiece.

I had an image in my head, and it was clear. I knew what I was doing. I'd done this before, a thousand times to be exact. Ten minutes later I had completed my masterpiece. I then went off to find my dad to give him my priceless artwork. He was busy playing guitar, so I just stared him down till he paid attention to me.

The drawing was of me, my brother, my sister, and my dad standing on one side of the page with a dog. On the other side was my mum and boy. She did not look happy. She had a mad face, one that you could see from across the hall, the one she uses when you've done something bad. It was because we had a dog, and she was yelling, "no dog!" at us. We all had sad faces, even the dog.

When my dad saw it, he started laughing so hard, but I didn't know why because I thought it was amazing and that is all that mattered to me, so I didn't really care. He then got up and went to show my mum. My mum was half laughing, but that other half she wasn't laughing had been because she felt very targeted. The drawing was also labelled *I love Dad* because I always labelled it either *I love Dad*, or *I love Mum* depending on who the drawings are for.

They then shut the door to the study because they were talking but I was trying to eavesdrop. I leaned against the door with a cup to my ears and my hands pressed against the door until they opened the door and I fell over. When I got up, I walked into the study, and I saw the drawing hung up on the wall and I was so happy. I went to bed very happy that night.

A couple of weeks later we found out we were going to the Hunter Valley. We thought we were going so our parents could go wine tasting but we were so wrong. We hopped into the car, my siblings and I squashed in the back of our car, my mum in the passenger seat and my dad was driving. It's only about a forty-minute drive so we decided we will survive.

When we arrived, we were kind of confused. This didn't look like a winery, no it was some little old house in the bush. My siblings and I kept bugging our parents to tell us where we were, but they just ignored us and said you'll see. We followed the little rocky path to the front door and rang the doorbell. After a couple of seconds, a lady answers the door and walks us through to her backyard. We were so shocked.

There were heaps of tiny little puppies! We were so happy. My siblings and I immediately rushed over to the puppies. The lady then asked us if we'd like to hold them and of course the answer was yes. We then went and sat down on her outdoor couch, and she brought over some little puppies.

The one I was holding was a little Cavoodle that was white with little spots of brown on her. My brother was also holding a Cavoodle that was a beautiful caramel brown colour. We would've spent all day with them. They were so cute and cuddly and who doesn't love puppies! but we weren't allowed too unfortunately. The lady took the puppies back to their little enclosed area and that's when we found the one. The little brown one that my brother was holding stayed away from all the other dogs when they were fighting so we knew he was the one. We then said our goodbyes and hopped back in the car with no dog.

We had a conversation on the way home about the dog because my mum still wasn't sold on that idea. So, we were discussing how us kids would need to help out because having a puppy is hard work apparently. I really did not think it was that hard, but I had to say what I had to say to get the dog. When we got home, we had decided that we would get him, but we needed to spend a week getting all the stuff we needed for a dog. We also needed to come up with a name for him. I was so excited all week. I could not sleep, I'd start jumping up and down randomly, and I'd tell everyone how excited I am. Every single day went so slowly. I just wanted it to be next week already. I couldn't wait. Then after lots of planning and shopping, we were ready.

We packed the car for our new little dog, Leo. We were ready to leave so we hopped in again. The drive felt so long because I just couldn't wait. I was too excited.

We finally arrived after what felt like forever. I could not contain my excitement. I just ran to the front door. The lady answered the door and was happy to see us back. I already knew where to go. I just wanted to see our dog. When we got to the backyard we were greeted by a bunch of puppies. The lady got our dog for us so he could meet us. We had no regrets with our decision, and we were ready to get him home. He said his last goodbyes to his family and to his owner then we hopped into the car with him. He sat on my mum's lap to make her love him because my mum still did not love dogs, but we were so excited.

When we got home, we gave him some water and a couple of treats, we put him in his little crate so he could settle in nicely. That was one of the best days ever.

Autograph:

Claudia

Biography:

Claudia is in year 7 at Novoschool.

The Sourdough Stall

Evie Furber

The glittering ocean rolled in and out of the soft warm sand of Corlette beach, clumps of seaweed dotting the sands like craters on the moon. The warm summer sun danced over the emerald sea making it sparkle as though it was filled with tiny diamonds. Large beach condos surrounded a small, faded, sunshine yellow house with a scrabbly green lawn with patches of brown. A large, beautiful frangipani with soft white flowers that were rimmed with yellow, its branches hugging the house, sat close to the footpath.

Up the footpath was a park. The park housed a large, wooden pirate ship that was painted an ochre brown, with a little red parrot perched atop the mast. Across the park there was a rope swing, woven like a basket. A kookaburra often landed to laugh on the swings top bar, their soft brown wings splashed with white fluttering as they adjusted softly.

All of that beauty, and my friends and I saw none of it, as we had eyes only for the people walking down the footpath. Most people were here for their holidays, but some were retirees who came for the peace and quiet associated with the beach that we were currently in the middle of disassembling.

As innocent bystanders wandered by, we shouted, "Get your sourdough here! Your tasty warm sourdough bread!" promptly disturbing the quiet and shattering the silence. Being the annoying (yet adorable) school kids that we were.

Some people stopped to survey the bread as one of my friends, Will, helpfully and happily supplied prices and advertisements. About one in ten wanderers actually bought something, with most of the people who passed by spinning tales about how they had forgotten their wallets at home even though we had the option to pay with cards or phones, but when we offered this information we were laughed off with dismissive compliments and excuses.

When there was a break in the flow of people, I went inside the house with another of my friends who was a year younger than me called Bethany, but everyone called her Beth. We were going to make lemonade for my brother Max, Will, and of course, ourselves.

I pulled a pot out of one of the drawers, which were the colour of washed-out eggshells as Beth grabbed sugar from another and bottled lemon juice out of the refrigerator. I measured out water from the tap and sugar from the cupboard for the simple syrup, the base of our lemonade. After mixing it I poured it into a pan and set it to a boil to dissolve the sugar, Beth poured the lemon juice into the syrup.

I had learned to make lemonade with my grandmother in her house in Brisbane. Going through the familiar movements brought forth a feeling of relaxation and belonging.

After a little while, the repetitive gurgling noise of the lemon juice pouring into the pot was just starting to get on my nerves. It finished and I diluted the lemonade with more water. I then grabbed my old blue jug and plonked it into the fridge to cool as no one likes lukewarm lemonade.

"Hey, where's my lemonade?" my brother called playfully as we wandered back to the stall.

"Still cooling."

"Aww," my brother's face morphed into an intense expression of conflict. He wanted lemonade now! But it was better cold, so he had to wait.

Waiting, waiting, waiting … My brother, Will, Beth, and I were all waiting for someone to come by. The waiting was not solemn but instead filled with laughter and jokes.

After a while I zoomed off towards the park, on my blue scooter, across the rough concrete path. Pushing with my bare feet felt like rubbing them on a cheese grater as I zoomed towards the pirate park by the beach. As I approached the warm familiar light of my favourite place to hang out with my brother, I felt joyful and excited, where the two of us would spend hours lying in the warm sun talking. The kookaburras flitting around me, flying from tree to tree, laughing all the way. Once reaching the park I scooted to a halt. I then pulled out a piece of chalk and roughly scribbled a picture of a loaf of bread and a quick advertisement of our stall. Then I turned and scooted back to get the lemonade out of the fridge so we could drink it. The others had sold another bread loaf while I was away. As we drank the lemonade, the brilliant, sweet taste blossomed on our lips.

After waiting about ten more minutes, we sold two loaves of bread to a kindly old lady. She was very sweet and after she left, we had sold all but one loaf of bread and most of our buns. The people out on their morning walks had all gone home, so we went inside to play a game of Evolution.

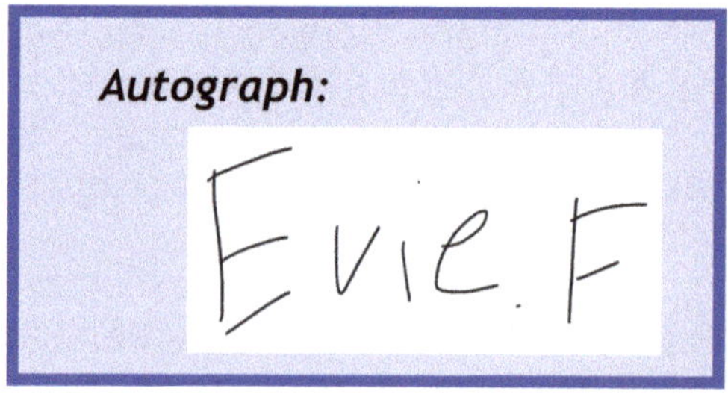

Biography:

Evie is in year 7 at Novoschool and was born in Sydney before moving to Melbourne when she was two. By the time she had turned four, she had lived in four different houses! Evie then lived in a caravan with her family travelling around Australia and New Zealand. While living on the road, she got her scuba diving certification aged 10, swam with turtles, spotted kiwis in the wild and stood on the very northern tip of Australia before settling in Newcastle where she currently lives.

Evie loves trying new things and her current interests include ice skating, aerial silks training, rock climbing, scuba diving, reading, skiing and exploring new places.

Fixing the Quad Bike

Jacob E.

I can hear my dad's voice yell across the yard as if he had a megaphone, and I can hear the sound of the quad bike roaring like a lion. I can smell the fuel and the sound of the dogs barking at the horse in the paddock and the sound of the wind whistling. I can feel the warm motor on my skin and the sun on my face. I hear the TV in the house, and the crack of a can opening.

My dad and I put fuel in the quad bike and put the battery in. I get on and turn the key, and I start riding it down the street.

The battery starts making weird and loud clicking noises, it makes a big popping sound, and the quad bike jumps forward and stops roughly. I wheel it back to the house and put it in the rusty old shed with hundreds of tools and lots of spiders. I take out the battery and find a new one. I put the new battery in and turned it on hoping that it would work.

It works! I jump up and down with joy.

I ride it around my eye burning green yard for 30 minutes. Then I get off to have a break. I go inside and I see one of my dogs, my big fluffy dog, Dexter, but I don't see my other dog, Rufus. I look around the house and I can't see him.

I look outside in my yard, but I don't see him. I look up and down the street. I don't see him, and I start to feel worried. Then I realized that someone left the gate open. He must've run out. I tell my dad, and we look around for about an hour, but no luck.

Then someone pulls into our driveway in a red car and three people step out and they have Rufus. I ran down as fast as I could with joy and excitement. I thanked them for finding Rufus then I brought him inside and cuddled him. I go back outside and clean the quad from all the mud that got onto the wheels. Then I paint it.

We eat chips, salmon and veg for dinner and then I watch Star Wars: Revenge of the Sith. Then I go to bed.

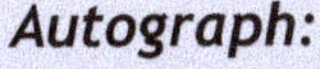
Autograph:

Biography:

Born in Newcastle NSW, Jacob loves gaming and 3D printing. He is always keen to try new adventures.

The Long Drive to Family

Jake Guest

When I think of the past I remember my road trips to Melbourne, filled with the joy and nightmares of long travel. My family has a Rav4. It is silver, with leather seats that always burnt the back of our thighs, and the confined space between us seems overwhelming during the long, dry, hot drive.

The car trip was too squishy with me, my brother Paul, Dad and Mum in our silver heat pack. I am relegated to the back seat in close confines with my brother. His constant clearing of his throat becomes infuriating fifteen minutes into the trip. I stare out the window and try to imagine myself as Julian in the Famous Five – the leader of the crew. My hopes dwindle when Paul ignores every instruction, I give him and scowls much like George as we listen to the next instalment of Blyton's imagination.

Mum was the provider of lollies, but she only gave us three or four an hour! Not enough to sustain us on a twelve-hour trip. Dad was the driver, audiobook cue-er and bad jokes provider. He chatted endlessly to Mum about the books he listened to, or critiqued the driving skills of those in front of him, while us, the stuck passengers, just groaned and listened on.

We loved visiting our Nana and Poppa. We'd go on this trip most years, despite having no time. Miles and miles of nothing, no games, no chatting. Just service station, service station, bush, service station, service station, bush, on and on … The landscape is as boring as the conversation in the car.

Finally, though, the bush opens up into rolling green paddocks. Poppa's farm comes into view; the luscious green paddocks, with cows slowly chewing. They stopped and stood to attention as we passed, chewing the air momentarily. And the brussel sprouts! So many brussel sprouts. They stretch out before me like the green lines of my poppa's freshly mowed lawn, symmetrical and straight, from far away. It feels exciting hopping out of the car into the cool Victorian air. Finally, out of the taste of Paul's atomic farts.

I enter the farmhouse. The warmth of Nanna's kitchen surrounds me; the smell of mouth-watering lasagne makes my stomach rumble. My Nanna smells like the kitchen, her smile warm and her perfume smells amazing, her hug feels like being surrounded in soft fairy floss. The smell of the dog's stinky fur tingles my allergies. She sits scratching in the corner which irritates my ears.

Poppa has so many cows and he also has a buggy that we drive around the farm with. The buggy is driven by me with the help of Poppa. We use the buggy to herd the cows but mainly just for having fun. My Poppa sometimes lets me ride the buggy on my own, which is super fun.

After visiting Nana and Poppa, we head home on the boring car trip again! The twist is we stop at Holbrook Bakery and eat delicious freshly made pies. The trip has its ups and downs but, in the end, it is an exciting time. This trip is amazing, but it's not the same as home. Though this means so much to me and my family because I love all my family even though we all share some quirky habits.

Biography:

Born in Newcastle, Jake grew up in the Hunter Valley and Newcastle. He has a love of many sports but mostly basketball.

My Last First Day

Jemma Gray

We all used to fight over the pole.

My best friend Maya and I never got the pole. But we didn't mind, as long as we were together. We both get each other and know each other like the back of our hands. The pole was where my friends and I sat at lunchtime. Only one person at a time could have the pole to lean on. Maya was the closest to my age which was nice since I was always the oldest out of my friends, I honestly don't know why being the oldest out of my friends bothers me, it just does. She is always really fun and great to be around, and she even understands most of the weird things about me! So, when I saw her on my last first day at my old school you would only be able to begin to understand how glad I was to see her again. I was like a brand-new puppy, when my humans came home from work and school to play with me.

As I walked into school that day, I saw the familiar area, with the old trees and the long line of bubblers right next to the canteen with hardly any changes since last year. Yet, I felt so different. I was in year six! With the familiar weight of the much-too-heavy-for-my-size backpack on my back. I saw her putting her backpack down, she had grown so much! Happiness spread through me as I called out to her at the same time as she called out to me, and I sprinted over to her.

"I can't believe we've finally started year six!" We laughed at the same time. "We get to run Funky Friday!" I gasped. There were clearly loads of people watching us, probably thinking we were so weird, but we didn't care one bit. I could feel myself shaking and going red with so, so much excitement! I mean like *year six!* Being with my *best friend!*

"And ring the school bells!" Maya added in, reminding me about the fact we were in the middle of a conversation, "And use the senior section of the library!" We laughed. I smiled inside, and probably had the biggest grin on the outside, it really was amazing to see each other again. You only get one year six, and you've got to make the absolute most of it!

We walked around the corner together, through the chatter and craziness of all the overexcited, jumpy kids that were so happy to see each other again, talking about the year ahead. I was a newly elected band leader for the year (yay!), and Maya was planning on running for SRC (student representative council). We really felt like this was going to be our best year of primary school.

The bell rang. We sprinted to the top cola to find out our classes for the year. Everyone was nervously waiting with their friends, hoping desperately to be sorted into the same classes. Maya and I sat together, hoping, waiting, for the announcement. It was time. We looked at each other. I nervously twisted my hair. I was shaking with a mix of excitement and nerves; would I get to be with my best friend? Or would I have to survive year six without her in my class? I don't think I would be able to handle that. One-by-one students stood as their name got called, looking around to see who was going to be their class.

Groups of friends squealed and jumped up and down, so excited to be in classes together. Some students stood alone, sadness falling across their faces when they realised that none of their friends were in their class.

Maya's name got called. We looked at each other nervously, hoping to hear my name too. Why did I always have to be at the end of the role?! It sometimes felt like eternity, the pain of waiting for my name to be called. We nervously waited, as more and more people stood up. My name got called. I stood up. I saw Maya grin from ear to ear. I did too. I was so happy I could cry! But of course, I wasn't going to, I was in *year six*. No matter what happened this year, we would be okay, as long as we're together. As I hugged my best friend, I hardly paid any attention to what teacher I was assigned, I was just so glad to be with Maya.

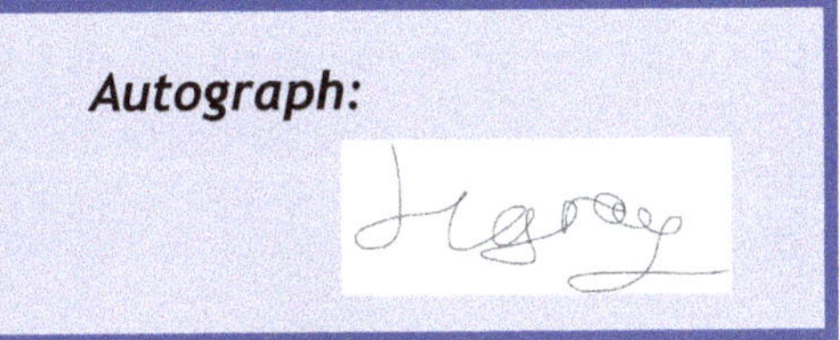

Biography:

Jemma is 13 years old, loves playing clarinet and enjoys a good book. She likes to go camping when possible and has a very excited dog called Milo.

Aunty's Spaghetti

Jesse Pankhurst

Every time my dad goes overseas or heads to a party or the pub, I always go to my cousin's house, where we're treated to the most incredible, specially made Spaghetti Bolognese by my aunty.

She's got the magic touch; it's hands down the best spaghetti I've ever had. The flavours are so rich and well-balanced it's like stepping into a savory version of candy land. Each bite hits you with a perfect combination of tender meat, hearty pasta, rich tomato, and just the right blend of spices. As it melts in my mouth, I feel completely relaxed. It's the warmth of this kitchen, of my aunty, that I miss about my mum.

***

When I was six, I used to spend hours playing outside in the garden. I'd chase butterflies and try to catch them, but they always flew away too fast. The sun would be warm, and I remember feeling so happy when I'd run around barefoot, my feet touching the soft grass. Sometimes, I'd pick flowers and give them to my mom.

She sits at the worn wooden table at the front of our house, steam writhing and curling around her face as she sips her coffee. Everything felt so peaceful, and I loved being outside, watching the clouds change shapes in the sky. It was a simple, perfect time.

***

My cousins and I wrestle and jostle as we all gather around the table, chatting, laughing, and bonding, while the TV hums in the background. The atmosphere is full of warmth, and we're all having an amazing time, savouring the delicious food and each other's company. Warmth fills my heart, and I feel relaxed.

Every time my dad said, "I'm going to the pub tonight", I knew I would be going to my aunty's house. I SPROUTED OUT OF MY CHAIR LIKE A BULLET AND SAID, "YAYYYYYY!" I can already hear my aunty calling my name and saying, "Dinner's READY!"

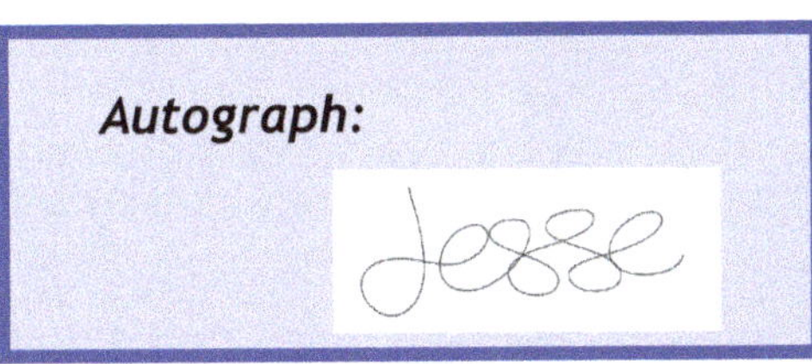

Autograph:

Biography:

Jesse is a 13 year old who loves the beach and summer. He is currently learning to play guitar.

The Most Fun I've Ever Had

Morgan P.

I was ten, maybe eleven years old when I went on my first cruise. My family and I were on a cruise ship near the Sydney opera house on the second day, during our one-week cruise vacation. My family and I had already eaten lots of delicious food, like burgers. Oh my, they were very tasty burgers. The sweet cold creamy soft serves made me crave for more and more each bite.

We moved into our rooms in the boat for the night and my dad and I played ping pong for the first time. My dad explained the game to me, and we played for ten minutes, with my dad winning most of the games, considering it was my first time playing. We lost the ball a couple of times – we were on the second floor, and it would bounce down to the lower floor. It made me feel kind of annoyed, like the feeling when you lose a valueless item and you're annoyed but at the same time you don't care at all about it, but then the other people on the cruise collected it for us which made me happy again. They would throw it back up and it would roll back towards us. It made it easier to get it.

My family and I also played bingo, even though it was illegal. My older brother Jacob won a bingo round and got $100. He probably put it towards his motorbike or something similar. He really liked motorbikes!

Me and my older brother Jacob were sprinting up a big flight of stairs, feeling jittery, fiddly and jumpy because at the top, a waterslide awaited me. Eventually, Jacob and I got to the top, and looked at the ocean. It was a beautiful view, with birds in the sky and boats in the ocean as well as really tall buildings with a humongous number of stories. I was also thinking about how high up we are and how windy it is compared to normal. The instructor explained to me how to go down, and I dipped just a toe, and talked to Jacob about it being cold. Eventually, I built up the courage to sit down and get used to the temperature, and the water gushed past me, slightly pushing me forwards. I moved forward just enough to start gaining speed at an alarming rate. Screams of joy came from my mouth and the smell of water filled my nostrils as I kept catching speed. Excitement and joy ran through my veins as dopamine filled my brain. I went faster and faster and faster, and suddenly, I reached the bottom of the waterslide. The thought that I wanted to go again immediately ran through my brain and body, like I just saw the sun for the first time, or I sniffed a flower for the first time in my entire life.

Autograph:

Biography:

Morgan is 12 and lives with my mum, dad and sister. He also has another sister and a brother. He loves cats and his favourite colour is pink. Morgan's favourite food is butter chicken and naan. In his spare time, he likes going to the cinema, playing games on his computer, and relaxing by listening to music while snuggled up with his favourite plushies.

When I Think of Road Trips

Otto Lucy

When I think of road trips, I always think of our family trips to Melbourne.

They were the works, twelve hours of intense togetherness, crammed into a car, breathing each other's air. One long day that both made and broke relationships.

The earliest trip I can remember was when I was three, maybe four. I was buzzing with excitement, my birthday was coming up, and being so close to Christmas meant double the presents. School had ended, and the days stretched out like open fields, slow mornings, secretly watching TV with my siblings while Mum and Dad snored in the other room. But best of all, it meant we were heading to Melbourne. It meant cousins. It meant the road trip.

My brothers and I were jammed in the back row, packed like luggage and fenced in like a game of Tetris. My sister, all eye-rolls and sighs, buried herself in a novel and pulled on her headphones as our "I Spy" competition got louder. Arguments broke out over colours and spellings, while Tom snoozed in the corner, a line of drool dangling from his mouth. Sleeping was his superpower; he was an expert.

Up front were my parents directly under the hot sun. The leather seats burned hot under the summer sun, practically melting into our skin. I could feel it through my toddler seat, sizzling beneath me. I wriggled around, desperate for a cooler spot, but luggage was everywhere –under our feet, strapped to the roof, stuffed in the pod. We were completely boxed in.

You might wonder why these road trips meant so much to me.

It was the people around me.

Mum, the self-proclaimed main driver, had long since banned Dad from the wheel. She couldn't handle his love of the fast lane. But the longer she drove, the more her road rage built, amped up by true crime podcasts that kept her awake and on edge.

Dad didn't mind. He sat happily in the passenger seat, charged all our devices, and passed back bags of lollies or blocks of chocolate. We devoured them like wolves as soon as they cleared the centre console. He was the calm voice to Mum's wild murder theories, his tone steady even as the podcast's suspense mounted.

Emma only took off her headphones to help teensy tiny me open snacks. The eight-year gap between us made her the most serious sibling, too old for fart jokes, too mature for the poking game that had us in stitches.

And then there was Max, my oldest brother, My protector, My bodyguard, My personal Uber for tired legs. We'd fake stretches and "accidentally" elbow Tom awake, just to laugh at his startled face. We'd laugh so much, those deep belly laughs that shook the car. That made everything feel light.

It was Max's warmth beside me, his arm pressed against mine, which made me feel whole. It was his laugh, the one that took over his whole face, that I chased. I would have done anything to hear that laugh.

And now, I miss it. I miss those games. I miss the early mornings of fun and cartoons and sibling chaos.

All we have now is the silence of adolescence.

Biography:

Otto is a vibrant kid who loves playing soccer and violin. He is 12 years old and lives in Newcastle. He loves visiting Melbourne, where he and his siblings were born, to visit his extended family.

Beach Party

Will Castles

On a sunny day I was with my friends on the beach having loads of fun, in my memory, it was perfect. Nice pristine water with waves just big enough to be good for surfing. The sand was hot and golden, and it burnt our feet like lava. I was with Harry, Edward, and Alex.

We had just started to go out into the water when our parents called us to wear sunscreen. We all groaned and moaned then went back, deciding we could hear our parents out for once. Finally, we could go out in the beautiful water, running at my top speed. I crashed into the water along with all my friends and then continued until we were 10 meters out, we started to throw the ball around and then played piggy in the middle, which was so much fun we played for thirty minutes straight.

After all that we eventually had to go back because we were hungry and then had sandwiches and cake for lunch. Once we finished, we played in the amazing water for what felt like short periods but was hours.

After all this we were worn out because I was only eight at the time and had played for four hours straight and it was now 6:00 pm and could now see the red skyline that had clouds that looked like fluffy marshmallows and I looked over at my friends, who were waving at me as they had to go home. I waved goodbye to them and went home as well. Shortly after that I hopped in our car and headed home, while reflecting on how much fun I had, still rubbing the sand off my legs.

Autograph:

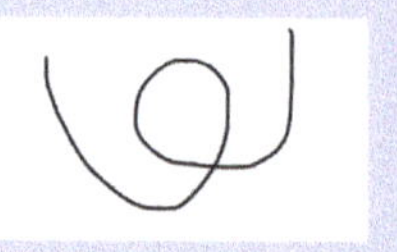

Biography:

Will is a 13-year-old Novostudent who loves sushi and caught a big fish off some breed once.

The Ride That Made Me

Zach Smith

My tires sliced over the pavement like a car on a mission. The wind lashed at my face, sharp and relentless, like a thousand tiny needles pricking my skin. I flew down the hill, pedalling harder, faster, unstoppable.

And at that moment, something strange happened. A wave of calm washed over me. It was as if fear had no right to exist inside me. I wasn't afraid. I was alive.

Then, in a blink, everything changed.

Crack.

My face slammed into the metal bar. The impact was sudden and brutal. It felt like being punched by the air itself. Pain exploded through my nose as blood blasted out of my nose like a shotgun, splattering the concrete in splashes of ruby red.

My whole face pulsed with numbness. My vision blurred and stung. I hunched over my bike, breath ragged, waiting - hoping - for the pain to fade.

And just like that, my mind took me back. Back to where it all began.

I was smaller, wobbling on a bright green bike. My dad was right behind me, holding the seat. His presence was steady and strong. The wind was gentle, brushing my cheeks like a whisper. I remember thinking, *I'm flying*. I loved that feeling of speed, of freedom. But more than that, I loved knowing Dad was there, keeping me from falling.

The sun glared off my handlebars, reflecting into my eyes. Sweat pooled under my helmet and trickled down my forehead. I blinked hard, heart racing, nerves building like a storm in my stomach. Over and over, I pedalled across the empty car park. Over and over, I fell.

But Dad was always there. Catching me. Lifting me. Encouraging me to try again.

And then finally, I got it.

I pushed off, planted my little feet onto the pedals, and lifted my head. I pedalled with everything I had. I leaned into the motion, steering, balancing, believing.

I was doing it, I was riding.

I was riding!

I was riding!!

I had never felt so fast. And now, even through the blood, even through the pain, I know why I ride.

It's not just about speed. It's about falling. And getting up. It's about remembering where I started, and never stopping.

Autograph:

Biography:

Zach likes fishing, playing basketball and hanging with his mates.

Section 2

Section Two:

Adventure

Warm Summer Memory

Archer Maguire

On a warm Sunday, I sit alone on my favourite swing that's suspended from a tall pail gum tree. There are other similar trees around. There's not much else except tall yellow grass surrounding me.

I hear a rumble of thunder in the distance; a big ominous black cloud is closing in on me in the distance. I get up and start to leave when I think to myself, what's the point of going? The storm might not even hit where I am. I sit back on the swing and start to watch the storm.

I remember making this swing, my dad had spent the last week making the beam to sit on. We had to sand and oil it till it shone like the sun. When the day came to put it up, we tied a piece of fishing wire to the back of an arrow and shot it over a branch. We took it in turns to try to get the arrow over. Me and my brother wanted to be the one to get it over. I tried really hard and so did my brother, there was a lot of yelling as we tried to have extra turns of shooting the arrow but in the end, it was my dad who did it. He then tied the rope to the end of the line then pulled it over from the other side.

The storm rumbled again but it was in the distance this time. A breeze ruffles my hair, and a feeling of calm comes over me.

Autograph:

Biography:

Archer is 13 and is the youngest in his family of four. He loves basketball.

Green

Astrid Wallace

I followed my family through the airport, the constant noise and movement reminding me of a swarm of clumsy, bustling beetles. It was packed with people on Christmas holidays, like us. We were all exhausted from the flight, plodding along slowly, my oldest brother, John, dragging his numerous ukuleles behind him, following the throng towards the doors.

As we grew closer, a feeling of anticipation ran through me. What would be different? How would it be different? We stepped through the thick, shiny metal doors, blinking against the warm sunlight.

It was so … green. Everything was green. Viridescent shades mixed and swirled together in a beautiful, luxuriant landscape, the grass sparkling like tiny blades of emerald, the trees alive with fluttering leaves of healthy, lush green, throwing dappled shadows across the terrain. Magnificent, vibrantly coloured birds flitted between the branches, producing a soft, sweet melody that swirled through the air, drifting up towards fluffy, pure white clouds.

The sky was an almost headache-inducing shade of bright azure blue, which only emphasised the greenness of the rest of the environment. I dropped my bags on the ground as I gasped, running towards the glorious sight in front of me – my energy suddenly rejuvenated. As I frolicked through the green, I seemed to forget the dull, dry, almost yellow foliage of Australia.

I laughed as I ran further into the trees, much to my families' dismay. We were already running late for check-in at our campsite, but I didn't care. I was soon surrounded by the tall, lush trees. I couldn't believe that we were so close to a city. This sort of green wasn't supposed to exist in nature, let alone the outside of some random airport.

I slowed, catching my breath. Looking back, I watched as my mum, dad, and John's girlfriend, Shelby, took the luggage from my brothers, sending them over to convince me to follow them while they found the hire car.

I glanced down for just a moment, but I soon realised that that wasn't long enough. Just in front of me was a small creek. I had seen creeks before, and they were murky and stagnant, the complete opposite of the thing before me. The water was fresh and crystal clear, shimmering like diamonds as it trickled downstream. Running water. I had never seen running water before. I stood, shell-shocked, staring at the stream.

"Come on Astrid," I heard my brother, Mark, call. "We have to get to the campsite before it gets too dark!"

"Plus, how will we ever get to the Ukulele Festival if we have to spend the whole time waiting for you to finish looking at the pretty plants?" John said as he took my hand and began pulling me the same way my parents went.

John was so excited about the Ukulele Festival that he hadn't stopped talking about it for the whole week. Last time, he was invited to go with some of his friends who also play ukulele, but this time we wanted to go on holiday as well.

As we neared the hire car, I glanced back for one last time, looking back longingly at the little pocket of paradise.

I looked away, surveying my surroundings. I froze, shocked once again. Maybe it wasn't such a small pocket. Everything was so overwhelmingly different, the plants, the animals, the sky, the water, this obviously wasn't just some new country. This was a whole other planet.

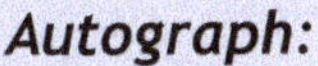

Autograph:

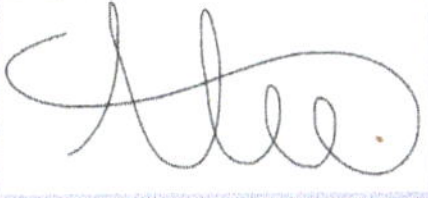

Biography:

Astrid is in Year 7. Her preferred habitat is the Jiu Jitsu mat and she can also be found exploring the various spheres of science or huddled in a corner reading a book. She loves shiny rocks, riding horses and stabbing her brother with swords on the fencing piste.

Expect the Unexpected

Bana Qattan

"Seat belts!" my dad announced with a note of urgency.

"Did we forget anything? Do we have everything? Charges? Suitcases? Airport food? Money? Did we lock the doors?" my mum exclaimed, rushed in words which created her cautiousness evident in her voice.

As I settled into my seat and put in my AirPods, I braced myself for all the experiences I was about to see, feel, and embrace.

I zoned out from my sister (Lara), and my brother (Zac), who was caught up in yet another sibling spat over how they wanted to sleep and are bugging each other. Instead, I succumbed to my own world, my music enveloping me as I rested my arms, cradling my face.

I love travelling; I do it every once in a while. Going to Malaysia was especially exciting, as it was my 13th birthday adventure, just a day after my birthday on the 16th. We were on route to the airport, the excitement buzzing in the car.

'*I can't tell where the journey will end, but I know where to start*'. Blurs of trees zoom hurtle past whilst Zac's neck is at a ninety-degree angle backwards, how do kids honestly have a burst of energy and a little later a sudden deep conversation with their snores and lassitude.

"BANA FINE I WARNED YOU!" she roars in my ear as she nicks my airpod away.

"Hey, what are you doing!?" I exclaim tugging on her arm whilst she teases me throwing her arm across the car.

"WELL," she says with an indication of targeting me with her voice and one of her million expressions, "if you were listening, you would know".

I tilt my head putting on one of my famous straight faces.

Ugh, why does she always exaggerate everything she says? I wonder with all the other internet browser tabs going on inside my head.

"Can I play with your phone?" she says, fluttering her eyes with innocence that's printed all over her face.

"Nooo, I gave it to you earlier, I'm busy." I say.

"Pleaseeeeee ok can I look through your bag?" she whines.

"Why would you even want my bag?" Scrunching up my nose and eyebrows as I catch her off guard and snatch my own airpod back.

"UGHHH fine" slumping her back and throwing her head back while her eye roll still needs practice on.

It was roughly 10:00 am, and our flight was at 1:00 pm. My mum was working through some forms for our flight when I noticed her face drain of colour and her heart drop.

"Oh. No." Her voice faded out whilst everyone's instincts turn on. "Both you and Lara's passports are just over a month expired," she said, panic and shock slipping into her tone. We were all caught off guard, unsure of what to do. In a flurry of phone calls, we reached out to our family friends, who were joining us on the holiday. They suggested contacting emergency passport services for assistance.

I couldn't believe this was happening; I had envisioned a relaxing day aboard the airplane. But then again, you always have to expect the unexpected. A true overthinker would know that.

The emergency services guided us to fill out an information form for both me and my sister. We had to rush to the post office to have our photos taken and tackle a mountain of paperwork. We dashed to Officeworks to print the necessary forms, snapping our photos as quickly as possible, adrenaline pumping. We arrived at the passport building, frantically getting everything signed, while they conducted checks on my sister and me. We sat there, patiently battling with desperation and sneaky hunger.

Fortunately, we received our brand-new passports within just 2-3 hours. With renewed hope, we checked all the flights, but everyone was fully booked

day,

after,

day,

after,

day.

Finally, we found a flight that could accommodate us, leaving at 11:00 pm that night. We updated our family friends and, in the meantime, spent time at their house. I tried to keep a positive attitude throughout the day, seeking distractions to ease my anxiety and mothering my siblings. While we were at their home, I felt slightly more relaxed, comforted in the knowledge that everything would turn out okay, even if no one voiced such reassurances.

Meanwhile, our parents were inundated with calls about refunds, cancellation fees, and financial implications. Pacing themself around the wooden floor. *'So wake me up when it's all over, When I'm wiser and I'm older. All this time I was finding myself, and I didn't know I was lost.'*

I distanced myself from those adult concerns and watched my younger siblings as they played innocently in the corner, blissfully unaware of the chaos surrounding our travel plans. I'm a thinker, not a natural talker, and my mind often spirals into overthinking, leading me to confront harsh realities.

Eventually, the airline informed us that since we had cancelled our outbound flight, they had sold our return flight for the 26th of April. Once they finally admitted that the words tumbled out of him, a desperate plea tinged with rage. "What?! How did you sell it in 2-3 hours?? Surely that's not accepted, we gave you no permission," he shouted, his voice cracking like a brittle branch. The phone felt like a weight in his hand, his knuckles white as he squeezed it. The next available return flight was scheduled for May 5th, which wasn't feasible for us due to school commitments and work obligations.

So we really tried but in the end the only possibility would be to understand that it can't work out for us, we understood that this could be a sign of safety and protection, that it wasn't meant for us, that we can't have fun because it will end up in pain and sadness.

That evening, we stayed at our friends' house, collapsing into a soothing sleep after such a tumultuous day. It was just what we needed.

'I tried carrying the weight of the world, But I only have two hands, Hope I get the chance to travel the world'.

"Thanks for all your help and for having us over," my mum said, a smile plastered on her face, masking the exhaustion and sorrow lurking beneath. This was an experience I never imagined I would encounter, sometimes you can't always get what you want or expect. As I put my AirPods back in, I daydreamed off into my own fantasy, contemplating the twists and turns life often throws our way.

Lyrics are taken from the song, "Wake Me Up", sung by Avicii, written by Avicii, Aloe Blacc and Michael Einziger.
Ref: Avicii Reveals Aloe Blacc Wrote 'Wake Me Up' Lyrics In Two Hours - Capital

Autograph:

Biography:

Bana is a 13 year old girl, and although she may appear typically young for her potential – the stars are the limit. She tends to be one of those people who is also everything, she enjoys lots of hobbies, she is grateful, and will help whoever, whenever, exceed herself as well as support anyone. Bana is not afraid of the tasks, challenges or storms ahead for she is "learning how to sail my ship".

Snow Trip

Benji Higginbottom

We drove in the car from home to Jindabyne. When we got to Jindabyne it was around seven degrees and windy. When we got inside we got ready to go to the pub for dinner I had a chicken schnitzel and chips with a lemonade, and then we went back to the house and went to sleep we got up in the morning, and drove to the ski mobile when we got there we opened the sky mobile with my friend Sibi and Jack, there was snow on the floor from my boots. The seats were black leather and soft inside. It was warm so the snow melted in about five minutes. Outside there was snow and rocks everywhere, there were trees covered in snow.

When we got there, I got out of the vehicle at the ski lodge and fell in a pile of snow when I got out. I brought my stuff into my room and we went to get our ski pass, when we got our ski pass we walked to the most easy ski area and we went down once and it was easy so we went to the black diamond ski it was the hardest one at Charlotte's pass and we race Down, I came first but my friend lost their phone down so when we back up we skied down and we got going on all the ski Slopes. Then we came back for lunch. We had chips and hot chocolate, it was delicious, then we went skiing some more and then we got called in for dinner. I can't remember exactly.

The second day we stayed inside until about 10:00 and when we went outside, we went on all the Slopes and for lunch we had sandwiches. We had spaghetti for dinner. It was pretty good. We stayed up until about 11:30 and then we went to bed. On the third day we went on all the Slopes all day. We did the rest on the last day. On the last day, I said goodbye to my friends, and we went to Jindabyne and stayed in a house there. The house was really nice, I got to stay in the master bedroom, because it was far away from my baby sisters who woke up in the middle of the night. Then we went back home at the end.

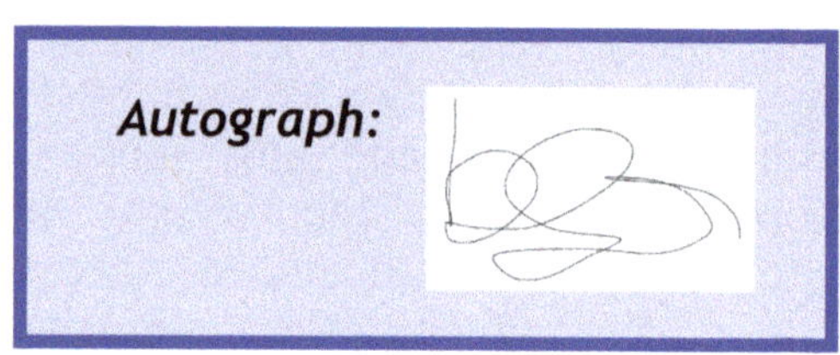

Autograph:

Family Road Trip

Frankie Clark-Jones

I have been attending the Gumball music festival since I was a chair and a half tall – so small and tumbly.

My sister and I would pack our bags the night before the festival, the set list would be blaring through my mini Megaboom. Zalia, stuck on repeat with her favourite dance moves – her only dance moves – a combination of weirdness and laughter.

We squished into our blue Mazda, with Mum strapping me into the booster seat, screaming my resistance to being contained. I hated that booster seat. I tried to escape for the third time, pulling on the door handle as we hurtled down the highway. When I realised I couldn't get out, I concentrated on making the hole that I had picked and stabbed in my seat larger – my only protest to being contained.

As a family, the drive in the car always goes like this: my sister Zalia gets sick, I sing to Mia Dyson, and my mums talk about BORING adult stuff.

My tummy grumbles, and my sister and I beg my mum to get Maccas, but Mum agrees to bean fries at Oliver's. From the back comes the chant "MACCAS, MACCAS, MACCAS!"

My mum's cave, and we pull into the drive-thru.

As I got handed my Happy Meal, I ripped the box open like a bolt of lightning. As I dig my hand in the box, I scream with excitement, seeing that I have received my very own Woody toy from Toy Story.

Distances ahead as we arrive, I feel the sound in my body more than my ears. The crowd scream and laughs joyfully.

As I see the smoke on the stage, it reminds me of roasting marshmallows with my family as it blows in my face.

There are so many games and music to listen to at the Gumball music festival. My favourites are the silent disco, face painting, and, of course, the loud music. My sister and I are running from one thing then another, holding hands as we run past all the people to find our way there. We are constantly rushing from activity to activity with joy like a cheetah hunting antelope, so much so that we have to create a plan of where to meet every hour, so my sister and I don't get lost.

All the times I have been here have been the most memorable times ever. I feel a closeness to my family as we build memories here.

And I can't wait to go this year, and next year. Gumball, here I come! I've already started listening to the set list for next year.

Autograph:

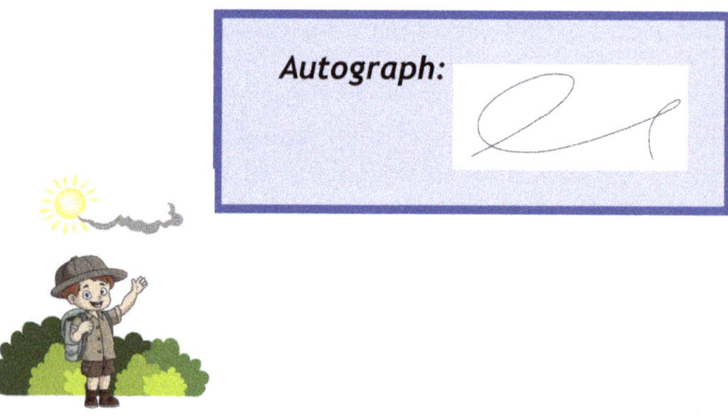

Biography:

Frankie is in year 7 at Novoschool.

A Disneyland Trip

Hugo Soliman

I was living in Washington, Seattle, for five years, with my mum, dad and two sisters. I was in sixth grade, and I was going to Australia because of my dad's work in late 2024. On the way to Australia, we stopped at Disneyland. When my family of five got there, it felt like we were at the start of a Disney movie.

There were a lot of people at the park. I felt excited and scared at the same time. The best ride was the Lightning McQueen ride. It was a rollercoaster ride. We sat down in a car and then the car started to move. Then we went through the story of Lightning McQueen, after a while we got to race another car and we went even faster. At the end it was a tie.

After we went on a Star Wars ride, we went on a spaceship (not a real one.) I was in control of how fast it went. My dad was steering, my mum was in the engine, my sisters were in control of the weapons. We fought the dark side, and we destroyed the dark side and won, it was really fun!

Then we had to walk back to the hotel, and we jumped in the pool. After that we got take away food every night and I got a quesadilla, and it smelt cheesy. My dad got a cocktail that went on fire. Then the next day we flew home to Australia, and it was a fourteen-hour trip, but it felt like a thirty-hour trip. The food was not good. It was so bad I nearly vomited on the food.

Autograph: 

Biography:

Hugo is 13 and goes to Novoschool. He has lived in America for five years and likes to play ping pong and basketball.

A Journey through Space, Time and Water

Jake Ivanovic Webber

I wake to the feeling of boiling hot sunlight on my skin, and the sound of the engine's explosive startup, the anchor's whining drone as it lifts. I hate being woken up like this. It is the most painful, annoying, and just a downright stupid way to be woken up. But knowing where we will be in a couple of hours, and the rocking of the boat in the waves, I slip back into dreamland.

Waking up a couple of hours later, the boat is silent, except for a soft creaky whining, which sounds like an insane chicken on drugs, and the soft occasional flap of the sails. I think to myself, sailing is so much nicer than using engines. I climb out of my bed, being careful not to trip on the big step down.

When most people think of a bedroom they think of a relatively large room with a bed, a small bedside table, some cupboards, a bookshelf, maybe a desk, and possibly a lounge.

On the boat, our bedrooms consisted of; a bed, a couple of drawers for clothes, a bookshelf, and a tiny area in the middle to stand; there wasn't even enough room for a chair. Most would think that this isn't enough room to live, and they would be right, fortunately we had a massive living room, for a boat at least.

Going upstairs, I see my dad, sitting outside in the helm chair as I walk past, he grunts a good morning, as someone can only do on five hours of sleep. I go into the cockpit and see on the screen that we have five hours left on the trip. We are going to one of my favourite places in the whole world, and I can't wait.

An hour later the sky darkens, and we spy a squall on the horizon. A squall, as I should clarify for all those landlubbers who are reading this, is a very short, and usually very strong storm, that mostly appears at sea. Whenever we see a squall coming towards us it usually goes like this: me and my sister run amuck on the roof closing windows and taking clothes off the line, while my parents try to reef the sail, while possibly putting the storm jib down. We then proceed to run into the lounge room, crashing on the massive lounge.

About one more hour later we see an island on the horizon, coming closer, we see the massive beach and the hundreds of boats there. We dropped the anchor, and after five long hours, we finally arrived at Whitehaven.

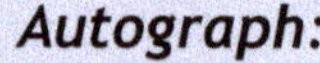

Autograph:

Biography:

Jake is 13 years old, and used to live on a sailboat. He enjoys cooking, reading, writing, playing with his cats and video games.

Universal Studios

Jeremy Murch

Two years ago, at Universal Studios, Singapore, there was a roller coaster I was really excited to go on. The human based on Battlestar Galactica and reaching speeds of 40 kmph. I was ready for it until I realised how fast it was and sent my sister up to see if she died. She didn't and I used fastrack to skip the two-hour queue and sat at the back of the roller coaster with my dad, not knowing at the time that all of the spots go the same speed. It started slowly gaining speed until rocketing up, climbing about 50-75 metres before going downward, sending us spiralling down towards the ground. I screamed until my vocal cords cracked and my stomach was flipping over and over and over again. This persisted for about a minute until we came to a halt. It was so fun. I then proceeded to ride the roller coaster nine more times in forty-five minutes until the park closed, and we left.

Another ride there was called Revenge of the Mummy. We lined up for twenty minutes underground in an Egyptian tomb hearing screams and light flickering around me.

By the time I was at the roller coaster I was terrified. I could not see but I took my seat and it started immediately we went backwards fast, in the dark and I thought I was going to die until we went forwards again down in the dark hearing screams and getting jump-scared until we went down backwards which is when I knew I was going to die until we stopped back at the start not dead knowing I would rather die than go on that roller coaster again.

I was in the line riding the Jurassic Park Rapids when I finally got on. I didn't get a raincoat since I thought that I wouldn't need one (I did). The ride was fun, being sprayed with water, spinning around and bumping into the walls. We then entered an abandoned facility, and I heard the sound of a waterfall. I knew what was coming, I braced myself and saw a massive drop, as we got closer to the edge my head started spinning not knowing what to do. We dropped down to the bottom, screaming the entire way down until we hit and my stomach flipped, leaving me wet for the next two hours. I never rode it again.

Overall, I loved going to Universal studios Singapore even though I thought I was going to die a few times. The adrenalin I got from that was worth it. My favourite ride was definitely the human ride, but I liked most of them a lot. You would have to give me millions of dollars to ride Revenge of the Mummy again, it looks fine until you are going down, backwards, in the dark at 40 kmph which scarred me for life and I now only ride roller coasters that I can see.

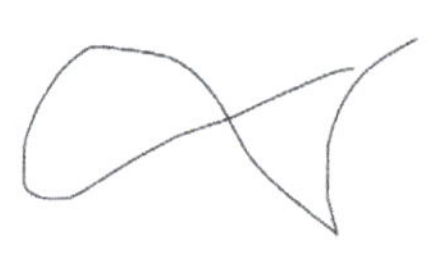

Autograph:

Biography:

Jeremy is a 12 year old boy. He enjoys cricket, coding and soccer. Some shows/movies Jeremy likes include Attack on Titan, Harry Potter and the Lord of the Rings.

How I Became an Amateur Radio Operator

Jonty H.

Until about a month ago I had no idea about a small but very active community of amateur radio enthusiasts in Australia and around the world. You may hear them referred to as 'Ham' radio users.

I have always been interested in radios and in communications more generally. I don't know why I always liked the idea of 'getting on the air'.

One morning as I was walking with my family in the local park, we met a man called Richard, and he was the president of the local 'ham' radio group in my area. Richard explained to me what it is and what he is doing, he was participating in radio 'net'. A 'net' is a weekly get together on the radio of 'ham' radio operators. The one that Richard was participating in was radio operators speaking from parks from all around Australia.

I decided that learning more about the 'ham' radio groups was something that I wanted to do, and so I decided to do it as my personal interest project (PIP).

That following week I went hunting for a club to certify me because you need a licence from the ACMA to operate it. I found a two-day course being run by Amateur Radio NSW (ARNSW) at Dural. I emailed them, filled in the forms, and sent them back! I was lucky and only needed to wait two weeks until the next course.

I spent two days learning about the radios, frequencies, aerials, and rules. I needed to sit two tests, a written test and a practical – I passed with an 88% on the written test and 100% on the practical.

After the tests I needed to get all the paperwork done and I chose my 'call sign' – my call sign was issued by the ACMA (Australian communication and media authority) and has to have VK (which stands for Australia) and 2 (which is for NSW).

The following week the local amateur radio club had its weekly 'net'. When it was my turn to speak, I used my call sign for the very first time. The first thing that I told them was that I had just got my radio licence. Everyone was so supportive and said how good it was to get new, younger amateurs to the group.

On Sunday evenings I listen to a news broadcast, this tells me all about what is happening in the amateur radio community including when there are get togethers or events. At the end, you can call in, called 'call backs' where people say where they are listening from. One Sunday, I was able to sit in the audio booth and listen as the news broadcast was being recorded, it was great.

Autograph: 

Biography:

Jonty is a 12-year-old boy who lives in the Hunter region. He enjoys heading out on his boat to fish and amateur radio. One day he hopes to get his pilot's licence, and to get his boat 'up and running' again and back in the water.

Me and the Ocean

L. P. Wood

The sunny blue sky stretches over me – boiling my skin. The waves crash onto the shore churning up the golden yellow sand driving the seagulls back and forth with the tide. People are everywhere, screaming, laughing and meandering around, swimmers filling the water leaving no space for anybody else and surfers owning the waves. I run out into the water, the energy of my excitement spreading throughout my body like a virus outbreak that is spreading around rapidly. I leap into the water diving into the cool, refreshing ocean water, the coldness of the water freezing my spine, the waves crashing against my body, as I swim further, and further, away from the shore.

I'm laying on my chest, it presses into the foam of the board providing what feels like a soft and smooth mattress. My Uncle Wade is laying behind me, his strong arms gliding through the water. I stare behind me as we paddle away from shore, getting further and further away.

up
I can't help but feel a sense of calmness as the waves lift us
and
down.
My hands glide through the water like a bird soaring through the wind.

I sit up looking out into the horizon, the salty smell of ocean air filling my nostrils, the shouts and screams of all the people on the shore muffled and muted by the vast space between us. The bright sun blinds my eyes.

I wait.

And wait.

Waves passing by each minute, and I can feel the weight of my uncle's head resting on my leg, his thick beard tickling my bare legs. I exhale, letting out a sigh.

I love this.

The quiet connection we have in this moment, between us and the surf. We all move together, connected and still. A symbiotic relationship with the surf as we wait for the swell. In the distance I see the monster gaining on us. Its large body grows bigger and bigger by the second as it gobbles up the ocean water, we turn around as quickly as possible and paddle our hearts out,

> my chest pounding
> > my breath heavy – and

> > my arms aching
> from the continuous
> paddling.

The monster grows closer and closer; I try not to imagine the monster carelessly munching us into a million tiny pieces and swallowing us into its bottomless pit of a throat and not filling its gigantic stomach the tiniest bit. The monster finally reaches us and gobbles us down.

We fly to the summit and get carried towards land. I feel the board vibrate and shake under my knees as I try to stand up, then when I build up enough strength to stand up, I jump to my feet. The water rushes and slices away from the board, the wind slaps me in the face.

I love this, the warm sun boiling every part of my body, the crystal-clear water splashing over me and my mum cheering from her board over the crest of the wave. Her screams boost my confidence, and I am grinning. As the wave ends, I jump off the board and into the water, the coolness of the water shooting a tingle up my spine. I pop out of the water with a smile on my face.

I turn around to look at my uncle, his eyes rimmed red from the salt water, his beard messy, his hair sticking up everywhere and a huge grin on his face. I walk up to the umbrella where my cousins, aunties, uncles and family are. They're eating salt and vinegar chips, my favourite. I sit down and plunge a salt and vinegar chip into my mouth crunching down onto the salty mess.

The heavy burden of the bat in my hands, I dig my bare feet into the sand, holding my stance steadily stopping the wind from pushing me out of place. All I can hear is silence, the sweet sound of silence. I look around people everywhere, children, babies, teenagers, parents, adults.

I try to focus my eyes on the bowler, my Uncle Wade, but it's hard for me to focus because of all the energy from surfing. It courses through my body making me feel invincible. I try to focus on how my uncle is going to throw the ball, powerful? Slow but curvy? A million questions flick through my head, but I can't settle on any – all I can see is that glassy azure ocean. I draw back my bat full of confidence, I build up all the energy inside of me from catching the wave, I feel the power channel through me.

The bowler launches the ball towards the stump, it comes straight to me, and I smash it as hard as I can like I'm trying to hit away a wild racoon that's attacking me. I watch as it flies into the sky, seeming like it doesn't want to stop. My dad who's playing as wicket keeper is behind me, complimenting my hit. I run towards the bowling line and back again. I do it again and again, effortlessly – grinning – before someone finally hurls the ball, ending my run. I look around at my family all clapping at my great performance, all smiling and happy. I look out into the ocean waves crashing, people swimming filling the water and surfers owning the waves. My people are everywhere, smiling, laughing. There is an ease in this moment. I exhale. Everyone is happy, just the way I like it.

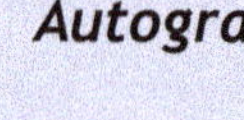

Autograph:

Biography:

Born in Newcastle, now aged 13, this author was a wise toddler, and is a loyal friend. He is a beach loving rock hopper, an engaged learner, and a keen chess player & mathematician, He is also an avid reader & rider, proud pianist, humble drummer, soccer super striker, basketball newbie, food connoisseur (no.1 fan of Mum's cooking), and just all round funny, polite, and awesome kid.

The Beautiful Bay

Lucy Fletcher

Anchorage is my happy place.
I love Anchorage.
I get to go here every year
on my birthday.
The beautiful bay
Curves around like a boomerang
The Vivid blue crashing waves,
echo across the bay.

The sand is hot and the water is cold.
The dolphins are splashing like my little
brother at bath time.

One hour is worth it,
just as long as I go.
The rooms are so cozy.
The bathrooms are as pretty as gold.

I tuck into my bed for
a good night's rest.
Just to only be awoken by my mum
"Happy birthday to you."
I rouse from my slumber,
to be greeted with presents.
A smile stretches out from my head to toe.
My mum makes the trip flow,
but my brother makes it slow!

At the end of the day in my special way,
I sit on the sand and look at the stars -
The dolphins splashing and flapping and crashing.

Oh how I love this beautiful Bay.

And when I haven't been in ages
I will beg and beg to go,
to my holiday home
Oh please can we go!

Autograph:

Lucy

Biography:

Lucy is a 12-year-old girl who likes hanging out with friends and going out. She has four brothers.

My Trip to Fiji

Saoirse McGowan

When I went to Fiji, I went snorkelling and I saw a sea snake and lots of fish.

My family and I went on a trip to Fiji last year, I have a key memory of snorkelling with my mum. This time last year, I was reading in my room on a Saturday morning, and my Mums came in with exciting news. They had been planning a surprise trip to Fiji. It was for us to go at the start of the Christmas holidays. My little brother and sister, my mum and I, planned out the trip together. I was excited because I had never been to Fiji, and I'd get to spend time at the beach. We did some research on places to stay, and there were lots of options to choose from.

Together, we decided on a place to stay, it was called Shangri-La. We chose it because it had many fun activities like kayaking, stand-up paddleboarding, snorkelling, mini golf, and inflatables on the water. We all liked the idea of the inflatables, they were set up as an obstacle course, and I wanted to try it out.

We flew to Fiji from Sydney. It was a four-hour flight, which I spent watching TV. I was really excited to get there and mostly excited to swim.

After getting off the plane, we went to the resort and checked into our hotel room. It was a nice hotel. I liked how it opened out onto a grassy area glowing in the warm sun, which faded into a beautiful beach with crystal clear water.

Once we settled in, we got food from the hotel restaurant, where I got hot chips. Then we got straight into the water, it was really warm, and we did a lot of swimming.

On the second day, we went snorkelling, and we saw lots of fish including some that were black with white scales near their eyes. There were lots of different sea creatures, and we even saw a sea snake, which I thought was cool. Later, I looked it up, and it was a poisonous one...

But in the end, it was a perfect holiday.

Autograph:

Saoirse

Biography:

Saoirse is 12 years old.

Discovering the Court
Sofia H.

This year I started to play Junior Development Series tennis competitions once a fortnight. I play mixed doubles socials on Monday nights. And now I have recently started to play Junior tournaments as well as getting coaching 1-3 times a week. The JDS tournaments (Junior Development Series) aren't my favourite because they are only one set (six games) and it is a sudden death deuce, but it is match practice. Since I am one of those players who needs the first set to warm up and figure out my opponent's game, the six-game match means I have to come out of the gates fast. This means that the opponent will most likely break my serve and hold their own, meaning I am two games down. When I first started playing these tournaments, I thought I was getting worse and it started to get in my head, it did not help my game. My mindset changed when I went to my first JT in a place called Picton.

I rocked up with my big bag and my new racquet. I was playing under 12s, which is what I am supposed to be in even though I usually play under 14s. I looked around, my legs were shaking, this was a whole new thing for me with three sets and new competition. What if I lose to a ten-year-old? What if I can't make it through the whole match? All these thoughts made it worse, I felt like I was going to be sick. I was playing a girl named Hermione. She had a slightly higher rank than me, I was a 1.2 and she was a 1.8, the first set flew by 6 games to 2 her way. I looked at the ground thinking about how much I would lose by, I then remembered what happened five years ago.

"What do all those numbers mean?" I asked with confusion.

"That is the score." My dad replied.

My dad was watching the final of the Australian Open and was on the edge of his seat, concentrating on every point. At that time, I knew that in tennis you tried to hit the ball with a racquet over a net. That was about it.

I then flicked back to present time.

"Love, one!" I called to the other end of the court as I looked down and bounced the ball on the ground.

The sweat rolled down my face and I thought about how far I have come in just a few years. Two games go by, and I am hitting so well. It gets to the tiebreaker, and she is catching up. I start to miss shots due to worriedness, and all the bad thoughts are starting to rush into my head, it looks like I am going to lose AGAIN, or I couldn't even hit a ball if it was the size of the moon. I try to ignore them and focus on hitting my shots, and to my luck, I win the tie-break.

It's a ten-point tie-break, I have practiced for this. 9-7 match point, to me. It's not over yet, "finish it," I say to myself as I hear my heartbeat in my ears. I feel my breathing speeding up and the entire point seems to go in slow motion. Game, set, match, I won. 2-6 7-5 10-7.

The next time I see Hermionie is in the consolidation round. It doesn't look like she wants to be there, her feet are stuck to the ground, and she is not hitting at her regular pace. I don't wish she had played like that when I versed her. I actually think that, if she had played worse then, I would have lost. That match taught me a lot, how to stick up for myself, to play at your level not the opponents, to not stress and how to win. Now I use JDS tournaments as a time to try new things, and I now know the JT is the tournament I like.

Over these years I have realised what I want to be when I am older... a tennis player, and the rest of my story ...

is yet to be written.

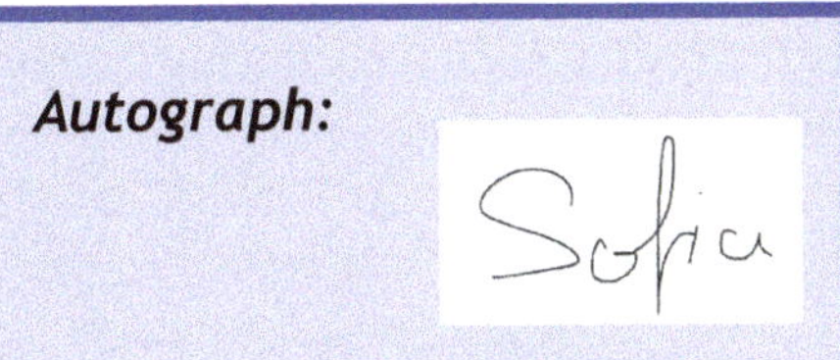

Going to New Zealand

Summer Kynaston

I had been waiting for this trip for two months, the calendar on my wall filled with more crosses every day. As the sun set, I got more and more excited as it got closer to the day we go on the plane.

The week before we went to Queensland, we had a hotel with a beautiful beach view and a restaurant in walking distance. We went for breakfast every morning with my mum's family. Every morning feet squished into the warm sand, and I went surfing in the salty sea with my two cousins Yadin and Lara. I really liked my mum's family.

The sky was orange and yellow and had pink clouds all around. After dinner we went to our hotel. I couldn't believe that this was the night I would be going to New Zealand finally. My dad had just gotten over being sick and had been sleeping all day. We think he had COVID. But luckily that afternoon he had joined us for dinner and was out of bed.

We went to bed early because we had to catch the plane at 3 am.

I could not sleep at all. I was way too excited. How long would we be on the plane, how big is the plane, how many people will there be, how long will the plane trip be? I tried everything to go to sleep but my mind was way too busy and excited. I laid there awake until apparently, I heard the alarm go off.

We all got up and gathered our bags to the van and as the sun came up, we drove an hour to the airport in silence. The TV called our ticket, and we gathered all of our bags up on the plane.

The moment I set foot on the plane was so exciting. It's like I finally made it after waiting so long. I was so happy. I felt like I was free, free from school from anyone judging me. Like I could do whatever I want, and no one would care. I love this feeling. When we finally arrived, I got out of the van and carried my heavy bag to the airport door. It was pitch black in the sky, but we could tell it was going to rain. It was warm and humid, and I took my giant fluffy jacket I got from an op shop in Queensland. I wore that jacket the entire trip.

I watched as my mum and my dad hugged for the last time ever. My mum started crying as she hugged me.

I was holding back tears as we left.

We carried all the bags into the airport doors, and I felt chills up my spine as I watched her drive away.

When we got in the airport it was cold. So many people were all trying to find their way to the next plane. We spent a while going through the security but to me it was fun. We felt lost and excited.

Once we had finally got to the spot we were meant to be at, I sat down on a seat. We had gone through security for what felt like five hours, but it only took one.

Autograph:

Summer

Biography:

Summer is a 13 year old girl who loves hanging out with her friends. She wants to live in New Zealand and have a dog named Nessie.

Curing Boredom

Theodore Murrell

It was a cool summer evening after school. Quinton, Dylan and I were sitting around, wondering what to do to cure our eternal boredom, when Dylan said we could try to make some money. All we needed to do now was think of how to make some money (because that's really easy).

It was about five minutes later when someone finally came up with an idea. Quinton said we could sell worm pee from his stinky old worm farm. Me, Dylan and Quinton were good friends, and we all knew each other well.

Quinton and I liked going fishing together. We would sit on the big jetty made out of concrete and that kind of grippy grid stuff that hurts like razor sharp oyster shells when you fall on it. We would sit and talk about the beach, what had happened recently at school or ... fishing.

Rarely, one of us would get a little fish tugging on our fishing line, but it didn't happen very often. When it did though, the excitement would be like when you find money on the ground and you want to pick it up before anyone else does, or in this case, before it snaps your line and swims away, then makes you reel your hookless line in with shame.

Me and Dylan were in the same class at school from kindy, all the way up until I moved house at the end of year four. We played soccer together at lunchtime before eating on the big sandstone blocks outside the classroom. I would go to his house after school a lot because both of my parents would be at work. We would go on bike rides around the block that he lived on, and we would always race down the hill. We would also play Minecraft on his Xbox or see who can do the most front flips on the trampoline. Dylan also had a quirky thing he would do when he sneezed. Whenever he sneezed it would always end with *"bllllllll llllllll llllllllllllll"*

Going back to the topic of our eternal boredom, we decided to go door to door, on foot, selling worm pee in bottles. Quinton's worm farm was full of worms, so obviously the worms would pee a lot. Quinton said that worm pee was good for plants, and he needed a way to get rid of it.

Like any living thing's wizz, worm pee is stinky, as you can probably imagine. It smells like mouldy dirt and well … pee.

Me and Dylan would stand back and hold our noses (Just like my little brother when he picks up my dog's poop) while Quinton poured the pee into empty juice and fizzy drink bottles. He would then dilute it with the hose so that it wouldn't be too strong for the plants and make them shrivel up and die like any plant that ever attempted to live in Dylan's garden … well, except for the weeds. They always seem to thrive in Dylan's back garden. And also because it makes more pee to sell.

We sold our worm wee delight over a few days after school and on the weekend. It didn't take too long before we had sold almost all of the worm pee. We added up all of the money and found out that we had made more than $100. We were thinking about splitting it evenly, but Dylan and I agreed that Quinton was the one that bought all of the worms and he was the one that looked after all of the worms, so we ended up giving him half of what we had earned before splitting the rest. We all had a lot of fun, and I think we would all definitely do it again.

Biography:

First generation Aussie born in 2012, Theo loves the surf, playing the drums and mountain biking.

This is why I used to sleep with the lights on

Tommy

Lying in my bed, staring up at the ceiling thinking about my importance in life. I turn around to see my pet cat, Lenny. My body shook faster than a drill. After I settled down, I let Lenny lie down on the bed and get pats from me for a little while, then I would have thought that there will be no more scares tonight, but I was wrong, VERY WRONG.

I woke up again, Lenny was not on my bed, however he screwed up my sleeping schedule. For a while I just sat on my bed, then I finally decided to go down the soft, but bumpy stairs to use the bathroom. I tried to be quiet since I did not want to wake mum up at whatever hour this is, walking back up the stairs my body felt ... Strange ... my guts were worried my head was getting a headache. I had no idea what was happening.

When I came back to my room, the bed sheets seemed different in a weird, rearranged way. I didn't take much notice of it, so I fixed the sheets and went back to bed.

I turned around again to peek into the living room, what was there I still have no idea, the best I could do to describe it is ... A dark shadowy figure just standing there, without a doubt I automatically do the old strategy of pulling the blanket and sheets over me.

With my face in my pillow, I hold it as tight as I can praying to whoever the heck I believe in. Then silence ... I stopped with my heart beating faster than a bullet train's maximum speed. I eventually gained enough courage to pull the sheets and blankets over! After I did that there was nothing there. How did this experience shape me? It made me interested in the paranormal somehow.

Autograph:

Biography:

Tommy is 13 and enjoys spending time with his pets, family and his friend Asher. He likes Lego, video games and urban legends.

One of My Favourite Memories

William Houston

I can remember the first time we went to have a look at the house. The bamboo fence on the sides, the quartz driveway, the rock path down the back to the massive sprawling tree.

Later on, we cut down the tree and got rid of the bamboo.

There was a downstairs. It was something similar to a workspace but filled with quirky items- a beer cap and a wheel. Later on, we made the room look nice. Soon after we expanded and built a deck upstairs. It looked nice. And when you walked in the house the lounge room was right there - you would find me, wrapped in my grandma on the couch watching a TV show.

Otherwise, I would be down the back with my grandpa digging for the newly arriving shed. Christmas was coming around and I was there with all my family. I got a Nerf pedal cart from Santa we still have till this day. They were amazing. We rode them with my cousin, all three of them.

I had another big present. It was a hoverboard with a go-kart attachment. It was amazing because I could Tow the Nerf paddle kart up the hill. We got a new driveway, and it went down all the way to the back at that time. I was going to race my motorbike. I had a KTM 65 from 2006 and I loved it, but I was too big for that bike now, so I had to ride Luke George's son's bike. It was a KTM 85. I loved it.

I was racing around the burm – it's like a motocross corner with the hill on it with a three-metre drop-off behind it. I had done this corner perfectly so many times it was easy, but my foot got stuck between the break and the footpeg and I crashed. I flipped in the air, then I crashed and broke my arm. I was in Maitland Hospital for eighteen hours just for them to x-ray my arm and another two hours to put a cast on my arm. They told me I had to have it on for eight months.

When I got to my grandma's, it was Easter. We had a great Easter despite my broken arm. After two months of owning our new house there was a house fire. We moved in with my grandma. It was amazing and lots of fun and I got to spend a lot of time with my family at my grandma's.

Shortly after we got a rental and moved out of my grandma's house. I would still go there to visit and stay over there for a little.

One of my favourite memories was when we got the pool and the spa. It was amazing. We got a lot more family members. Grandma's house was the second option we could go to. I have lots of good memories at that house and made a lot of new friends, but mainly being at grandma's house and memories with my grandma and poppy were some of the best memories.

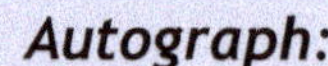 **Autograph:** 

Biography:
Will enjoys Motocross and bike riding.

Section 3 - Games

Section Three:

Games

Kaifun

Helena-Jean Anderson

I was six years old …

When we go to Friday nights at Kaifun for dinner with my friends.

Queenie started counting.

"One two three …"

Queenie is one of my friends, she is really kind. But is really good at games, even when she goes easier on us, she still wins. Queenie is three years older than me and loves spider man. I always think she will turn into Spiderman because she knows everything about Spiderman.

So Sofia, Judey and I hid silently between two walls, our feet in squishy, murky, ankle-deep water. Pouring. Heavy. Rain runs down our face,

     gathering,

          bouldering,

               sticking on to our

eyelashes.

Our clothes and hair feel like it's turning into our skin from the rain. Our hair is darkening from blond to midnight black every second. The cold rain running down our spines.

I heard the sounds of people eating rice and talking cheerfully. Right to us. Judy used to signal us to be quiet. When we are next to tables where people are eating, outside but under shelter from the rain. After a few games she didn't have to anymore.

Something slowly started creeping in, making us cull. making our shoulders comes to our necks in fear. Making us hope harder we won't be found.

We tip-toe like ninjas, but as slow as sloths until we get to the other side of the narrow metal wall path.

No talking, no whispering and certainly no banging into the metal walls. It sounds like dropping a metal drink bottle in a test, vibrating until all the eyes are on you.

But Sofia never stayed quiet for long. She would ask thousands of questions. Like how much longer, when will food be here and are ants the smallest insect. She had a four-year-old's curiosity. But she was our spy. Sofia is fun and sassy. She always gets away with the sassy because she is four and is always wrong. Sofia would make you do that under shirt hold in your laugh that turns into a giggle. Sofia is short enough to see under the metal fence, to tell us where Queenie was looking for us.

We got to the end, a garden where two massive trees arch over our heads. Its leaves are olive green for a long while it was one of the greenest trees I ever saw in Phon Phen. We stand or sit behind the green tall olive trees and bushes. In front of us is this short wooden fence with planks going across it making gaps for us to slide through. I always stand behind the trees because it is easier to hide there. Sofia sat behind the bushes in the mud.

"My clothes are dirty," Sofia complained.

Judey stands behind the tree closest to the walls but also closes to the fence, in case Queenie comes.

Judey is the one with strategy, always the hardest to find. She is one year older than me. Judey loves facts about space and is really good at math and sport. If Judey starts in, she knows every good hiding spot. So, it is very good to hide with her, but really bad if she starts in.

You can never see anything properly. The only lights there you get are glistening jaw dropping fairy lights that hang over our heads. Making it the most beautiful thing you've ever seen.

No one can hear what anyone is saying because of the loud blast of Khmer songs in the distance. I can't speak Khmer, but most of my friends can. My friend's parents and my parents have to shout just to talk to the person right next to them, all while trying to enjoy a nice fried rice dinner.

Soft quiet footsteps, looking for us. We sprinted to camouflage behind the trees. Sucking our bellies in.

And holding our breath like it is our last.

Hoping,

      wishing,

           wanting success.

I know I can't hold it any longer ... My stomach is echoing from the smell of food it's torture.

Queenie comes toward me, and I slowly circle around the tree, matching her footsteps. My feet step into the wet, cold, murky water as I move carefully, trying not to make a splash.

However, Sofia doesn't copy me fast enough. "Found You!" Queenie screams at the top of her voice.

Sadly, now Sofia is found. Her top priority now is to make sure that I am found. Till, the dreaded words are spoken ... "Found you!" Queenie and Sofia's voices echo in the back of my head.

But Judey is gone, she somehow sneaked through the fence and found a new hiding spot. Without being spotted, by me, Queenie and Sofia.

We looked everywhere; we came back to the same spot just to figure out she never left. She says, "It's strategy". I think it is just luck.

Hide and seek is always so hard with my friends. The way Sofia ensures we fail, how loud both Sofia and Judey speak, the way they all of them, always make me laugh until I cough. How quick Queenie can find us, that I still think she is Spiderman in disguise.

But even with the backstabbing, I wish it would last forever.

Autograph:

Biography:

Helena-Jean's favourite colour is shortbread yellow. She likes pizza and sushi. She has a pet rabbit named Carrot. Her favourite movie character is Bob the minion. Her favourite TV show is Brooklyn nine nine. She likes camp fires and roasting marshmallows.

Card Games

Myles Upton

The table was piled to the brim with Uno cards, reaching higher than the clouds. The floorboards struggled to hold all of the reverses and wildcards slamming the table. The walls felt like they were caving in. Our valuable cards hid in the trenches of the battlefield, waiting for the perfect moment to strike. It felt like millions of cards were being placed at a time, each card that got placed increased the tension of the game and the hatred we torched into each other. This used to be a fun family game night, but now it's turned to a violent and bloodthirsty war, we always forget what it's like to have fun on these nights.

I protected my final card like a valuable jewel by cupping it onto my chest and glared at my opponent's hand.

My fingers wrapped against the back of the card. Sweat dripped down my eyebrows as I watched my brother scroll through his card options. His hand floated through the air, looking for options like a vulture looking for scraps. He picks up from the loose toppling pile. It's fine, I can wait for his next turn. He scanned his new card but then slammed it back down into the discard pile. It was a wild card. Blue. I looked down into my hand, A blue five. This was it, this was my opportunity. I was about to win. After gruelling hours of destroying my enemies, I was about to come victorious. The war would be over, and I would come out with bragging rights. I took the final blow and placed down my blue five. Whines and groans floated through the air, followed with tossed cards flying in each direction like ninja stars. My brother was especially mad. His loud crying screams filled the tension and silence left in the air. They don't call me the Uno Shark for *no* reason.

My face lights up in the glaring light. My eyelids are heavy, my fingers have started to unconsciously sink into the keys. The sound of the clicking hypnotises my mind, and the blue light reflects onto my face, lighting it up like crystalized water on a sunny beach day. I push my chair out using my desk for a boost. My legs hobble to my brother's room and nervously open the door. I am met with a whine that bounced across the walls and a scrunched-up face looking in my direction. I begin to ask him if he wants to play some sort of game but get an instant rejection.

I meander back to my room and face plant onto my bed, almost squishing my fat calico cat. My gears stop moving and my hope depletes. I extend my arm to pet her chubby face but are greeted with a swat and a bite instead. I instinctively grab her string toy and start to sway it in front of her face. Her pupils widen and she begins to swab and nibble on it. At least I still have her to play with. A smile trickles down my face as she jumps into the sky to try and swoop the string down. A part of me wishes that my cat was my brother, but I know that I won't be able to drag him out of his room, so I continue to swing it in front of her face. Eventually she gets skittish and dashes away onto her mighty cat tower. I can reach her on top of her cat tower, but I could tell she just wanted to be left alone. I hobble back to my room and swing around in my chair. Footsteps began to creep up to my room, but I didn't think much of it. I begin to turn on my computer until I see a familiar face at the door. It was my brother.

"Do you want to play Uno with me?"

Autograph: M.U

Biography:

Myles was born in Newcastle. Since then he's done karate, played soccer, won a Spelling Bee and visited Japan. He hopes to do lots more things.

Life's Not Fair

Rochelle Smith

Being the youngest of four children, I quickly got used to the fact that life's not fair.

I was expected to know the rules without being told. Everyone presumed that someone else would have told me or that I would have learnt somewhere along the way, and so the time a swear word slipped out, I was reprimanded harshly – even though I didn't know it was taboo.

I missed out on a lot of rites of passage; childhood experiences. By the time I came around, my parents had decided that the Easter Show was for little kids, and so we didn't go as a family; despite the fact I was desperate for a showbag.

And don't even get me started on the hand-me-downs. My first day of high school, when I knew no one, I arrived in a faded tunic that looked like it could be from the time of the dinosaurs. Talk about making a first impression. Like I said, life's not fair.

My family were always massively into games: Monopoly, Settlers of Catan, 500, Risk, Nightmare – you name it, we probably played it. When I was much younger however, a lot of the strategy of these games were out of my reach, and so a simple game like Uno was perfect for me ... while also becoming the catalyst for an evil scheme.

To say my sister is competitive is an understatement. She will do anything to win, even in the most nonsensical of situations. Like making sure she got the last kebab, or throwing furniture in front of me as I'd chase her during a game of tips – many an ankle was sprained during these activities as a result.

Her competitive spirit knew no bounds – and this was most evident with the great Uno debacle of '97.

Everyone knows that the best card to get in Uno is a Draw Four Wild, followed closely by the Draw Two. This is the regular, original Uno I'm talking about – invented well before the Internet and the fall of the Berlin Wall. Apparently, it was developed by a man who couldn't stop arguing with his son about the rules of another card game, so just made his own. Sounds like an extreme reaction to a disagreement if you ask me.

Well, my eldest sister wanted an edge in the game, and so, without me or any of my other siblings knowing, put a tiny rip in every Draw Four and Draw Two card to assist in her cheating exploits. Usually, the game was quite fair without any issues, but suddenly my sister became unbeatable … in a game of chance. Now, yes, it is true that you could find it comical that we didn't realise. I think we never thought our sainted older sister would do such a thing and just assumed the pack was starting to get old. This probably went on for a few months – honestly, we should have got suspicious when it was all she wanted to play.

Then came the day my cousins came over. Being a little older and wiser than me and my other siblings, they immediately noticed, "Why are all your Draw Fours and Twos ripped?" And suddenly it dawned on us – what our scheming sister had done. The betrayal hit deeply. I'd always looked up to her, had her on a pedestal and in a moment, the years of respect I had for her came crashing down. For the first time, my sister was just human. My eyes were open to the truth, and I don't believe it's ever been the same since. She's now my equal whom I can question, argue with, and thankfully, win against.

A few smacks and a grounding later, we stopped playing Uno. My sister became a surgeon, and, I must say, it fills me with some sort of nefarious delight that she spends her days neck deep in other people's colons. That's karma for you. Interestingly enough, the cards were kept and sat unused for many years. Until of course her children came along many moons later and wanted to play a game ...

Autograph:

Biography:

Rochelle grew up in the heart of Sydney, where her family's deep love for literature was matched only by their fondness for lively Maths quizzes at family dinner.

Rochelle teaches STEM at Novoschool

extract from the school website

A Rough Game

Scarlett Melling

Grey clouds pressed down onto the sky, threatening to break through the shield. I was talking with my teammates before an intense rugby match, feeling disgruntled by the lack of kindness and praise radiating from my teammates. The opposition turned up to the fields and my mind got blurry; scared by the big girls that were going to fight for the ball with all their might.

We made our way into the locker rooms to prepare for the long game ahead of us, energy of bravery and excitement washed over the team as we played music through a speaker. Singing echoed and an energy of acceleration made its way through the air as we taped up our shoes, so we didn't have to tie them back up in the middle of the game.

After we did our team's chant, we lined up at the door of the locker room, I was always at the back of the line, I was always on the bench, and when I was on the field, I never had gotten the ball, as much as I called out for it.

As we had run onto the field, the boys' team was clapping us out, we lined up to shake hands with the opposition, I knew most of the girls because I went to the same school. Being generous with my smile, I glance across at them.

My mouthguard was stuffed in my sock, I had to sit on the bench with my teammate as the game started, I didn't understand how the girl who played soccer before playing rugby was on the starting lineup.

I always had been so nice to my team, but it was never reciprocated. It always felt nice to yell from the sidelines and praise them for good tackles, passes, trys or kicks.

When I had finally got called onto the field, the dreary sky cleared up and adrenaline rushed into my veins. When the opposing team approached with the ball, I went up to make a tackle, but instead I was on the ground, rolling on my neck. A small pain went through my back, but I immediately stood up to get behind the referee with the rest of my teammates. The next tackle that was made was by my captain, a strong girl with a temperate attitude.

As the game moved more on, I had a small metallic smell from my nose, and my head felt slightly dizzy. As I got taken off the field, I talked to the team's medic, he told me to rest it up and he got me some ice. I stayed off for a bit before I felt up to fighting for the win again.

A little further into the game and I made a couple tackles, with the help of my teammates. Goals were made by my captain, earning us extra points. By the time the game ended it was 24-8.

We had won.

When I celebrated with my team, a smile crept onto my face, as we grabbed water bottles and did our winning chant, spraying water all over the locker room.

We had won!

By the time we got ready to go home I hugged some of my teammates and wished to see them at training. When I got into the car we immediately went to KFC, tradition for a winning, or a lost game.

Scarlett is 13 years old. She enjoys musical theatre and hanging out with friends.

First Steps

Sue Hatfield-Smith

In the photo, darkened by poor lighting and the sepia tones of the technology of my childhood, he is standing up – grinning. It is broad, and real, and almost reaches to the end of his being. It's the grin of childhood joy. My older brother and I beam at the camera clearly enraptured by his bliss, applauding his momentous achievement. But my little brother is grinning at us. He is oblivious to the camera or the social etiquette of smiling and posing. He only has eyes for us.

It's the earliest memory I have of him; I'm not even sure if it's a memory or if it just feels like one from all the times I have stared at that photo – recreating the moment from the fragments of my mother's voice, tickling my ear. It's the story I feel now, of the love I know for my brother.

It's that same love but bigger, fiercer that swells inside me when I see him dipping his head, hiding his tears at school. The local idiot that catches my bus, smug beside him. He terrorises everyone with his stupidity but today he has turned his focus on my little brother, tackling him backwards over a chair. Being three years older than my brother, he sees an easy target – and I see a coward. My ferocity reverberates in my older brothers' eyes as he strides across the barren oval towards me. His face is stern with worry that bleeds into anger, and God knows he is quick to anger.

It's an anger that I have seen explode during many a family football game and resulted in him kicking the football as far as he can down our back paddock.

It is an anger that has echoed in my ears when we played our favourite game of "Who is faster?" A game that in its entirety was stupid and dangerous to an adult, but as a child was exhilarating with danger.

As soon as we got home from school, while we waited for our parents to get home, one of us would jump onto the quad motorbike that our parents owned, and drive to the high point of our paddock. A track was well worn from there – down through the paddock to the lowest point. The other two competitors had to hold onto the hard metal frame that wrapped around the back of the bike, designed to hold cargo on, and run. Run until your legs no longer felt like they are attached to your body and the fear of letting go of the cargo carrier becomes all too real, all too late. The driver's job is to speed down the hill, yelling loudly into the wind, oblivious to the ensuing carnage playing out behind you.

The last person holding on was of course "the fastest", and the other competitor usually ended up not only the loser, but seriously maimed, as their legs had spiralled out of sync with their body on the uneven ground, like a Road Runner episode. My older brother was not only older, and by default thought he was better, but he was also faster than both me and my little brother ... except when holding onto the back of this bike. Something about having stationary arms meant that his legs couldn't find their rhythm and he would fall early. My little brother and I were not gracious in our victories either. With few opportunities to one-up him, we loudly relished this moment, every time. And like a pressure cooker – he would explode.

It is this anger that has been refocused now though, towards the idiot. But I have already beat him to it – the bond between myself and my younger brother unified through all those small motorbiking victories and forged through the combined inability to live up to the standard set by our older brother. It's *my* hands that grab that kid's shirt with a ferocity that is surprising to me, as I shove him so hard that it shakes me. I do not think of his size, his mates, his dark cynical need for retribution and cruelty. I think of my brother's face beaming at me as he took his first steps, full of belief – in me. I feel not only my energy surging and swelling but that of the group that has gathered around me, pressing in on us, ready to put up the chant, "fight, fight, fight".

"Touch him again – go on," I taunt the idiot. I glare upwards into his dark eyes and step in close to him. So close, I can feel the hot stench of his breath on my face, and see the slight snarl in his top lip, like a cornered dog. I was small then. My older brother was smaller again, but I could feel him behind me, tense, poised. Waiting to see what would happen. My menacing anger rolled out of me like a fortress – shaking the perpetrators' foundations until he crumbled, looked around at the growing crowd and skulked off.

I looked over at my little brother – he nodded indistinguishably at me, as his eyes welled again. I wanted to stop and sit with him then. To cuddle him, on the oval in front of the whole school, like we had cuddled when he couldn't hold onto the back of the motorbike – fell and twisted his ankle, or when he bounced off the front of the motorbike, so quickly that I couldn't even slow down before I ran over him catching his spine on the axle as it bounced over him – the same injury the idiot had just antagonised, or how we did when we laid on the trampoline gazing up at the night sky, telling small profound truths about ourselves that made us feel less weird and alone in this world. I wanted to cuddle him like that day when he took his first steps, beaming at us. But he was new to high school, and new to the cautions of social influences. He was no longer oblivious to people's opinions around him, carefree and totally in the moment. Now he glanced around, cautiously, quick to wipe the tears before they fell. And I turned and left him with his new friends whose approval he now sought – not mine.

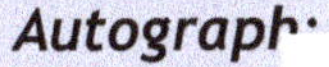

Autograph:

> **Biography:**
>
> Inspired by her relationship with her own HSC English teacher, Sue realized the power of literature to transcend time, allowing us to meet ourselves in other peoples' stories.
>
> Sue teaches Humanities at Novoschool
>
> *extract from the school website*

The Console

Theo Radvan

In the warm, comforting glow of the ceiling light of my home, I am cooled by the swift breeze of the air conditioning flowing through the rooms and the walls, my fingers twitching and snapping to the movements and correlations of the joystick on my Nintendo Switch. Anger boils in a pot deep, deep down in my heart, and it boils and boils and boils through the unfairness of the game I am currently playing, and how much better everyone is then I am! But through sheer will and determination, I blast through the competition, barely making it to the end in time. And the water boiling inside of that pot? Well, it becomes the key ingredient of a sweet, tasty soup. Looking at the Nintendo Switch I have had almost my entire life, it takes me back, way back to when I was first given it by my dad.

It was nothing but an ordinary day. I was incredibly young, maybe four or five I am pretty sure. I had just gotten back from kindergarten when my dad walked up to me, his Nintendo Switch in his hand.

The memory is a little bit foggy ... but I think the words he spoke were along the lines of;

"Hey, I found my old video game controller, and I want you to have it, because it is old and dusty and I have moved on to other things."

I did not know what a video game controller was at the time, other than a few rumours and some people claiming they had one.

"Hey! Hey! Guess what I just got!!!" They would brag and their friends would reply;

"Yeah? What, What??? Tell us!" and they would go on a long ramble about the new Nintendo Switch they had just been given. I was so confused and intrigued back then, wondering, curious about what they were talking about, constantly every day. But from the moment I flicked the power switch on, I was so excited and curious about what was to happen! But when the screen lit up for the very first time, revealing nothing but black darkness for what felt like forever, I started to get nervous. What if it didn't work? The logo faded in, showing that this was in fact, itself in the flesh ... I realised something, something bad ... I still had to make an account!!! GOSH DARN IT!!!

It took my dad quite a while to create my own account. It felt like I would never get to use my new console, but after what felt like years, he figured it out.

I booted up *Mario Kart 8 Deluxe* for the very first time, and I was immediately hooked on the game. I would play it all day round with my parents, my sister, and very rarely online. I HAD to win this race! My dignity was on the line here!!! Every race felt like a sweaty competition with the clock, every turn and trick, they all had to be PERFECT. But sometimes ... It feels like my finger, my hands, and my brain were just ... calculating decisions themselves ... Like they had a mind of their own ... We loved this game. Racing and driving and throwing shells at each other, slipping on bananas someone threw onto the ground two laps ago, pushing each other around and having WAY too much fun then we should have. Furious at each other when we wouldn't win.

I still remember when we would argue over which track to play. My sister really liked the rainforest one with wood and planks. My mum liked the one that just went in circles. (Booooring ...) And me? Well, as every eight-year-old boy liked, I adored Bowser's Castle. Because it's sick as hell!!!

Also, Blue Shells.
Screw.
Blue Shells.

I look down at my Switch. These moments were what shaped me, and my love for video games. Nowadays I have almost sixty games on my switch, and I remember when I had almost none. My mum calls out for dinner.

"Coming!" I turn the switch off and I look into the blank, black screen. Sometimes, I wonder who I would be if I hadn't been given this at all. I am glad my dad gave me this Nintendo Switch, as I would for sure not be the same person without it. Ever.

List of Authors

Alexander Lindsay

Archer Maguire

Astrid Wallace

Bana Qattan

Benji Higginbottom

Claudia Sim

Evie Furber

Frankie Clark-Jones

Helena-Jean Anderson

Hugo Soliman

Jacob E.

Jake Guest

Jake Ivanovic Webber

Jemma Gray

Jeremy Murch

Jesse Pankhurst

Jonty H.

L. P. Wood

Lucy Fletcher

Morgan P.

Myles Upton

Otto Lucy

Rochelle Smith

Saoirse

Scarlett Melling

Sofia H.

Sue Hatfield-Smith

Summer Kynaston

Theodore Murrell

Theo Radvan

Tommy

William Houston

Will Castles

Zach Smith